The Franklin's Tale

Geoffrey Chaucer
The Franklin's Tale

Retold by Ian Serraillier
Illustrated by Philip Gough

KAYE & WARD LTD/LONDON

FREDERICK WARNE & COMPANY INC/NEW YORK

First published in Great Britain by
Kaye & Ward Ltd
21 New Street, London EC2M 4NT
1972

First published in the USA by
Frederick Warne & Co Inc
101 Fifth Avenue, New York, NY 10003
1972

ISBN 0 7182 0924 9 (Great Britain)
ISBN 0-7232-6092-3 (United States of America)
Library of Congress Catalog Card No. 72-79498

Printed in England by Jarrold & Sons Ltd, Norwich

Introduction

The Franklin's Tale is one of THE CANTERBURY
TALES, the most famous work of the earliest of the great
English poets, Geoffrey Chaucer (1340?–1400). The
Franklin, a hospitable and well-to-do country gentleman,
tells the tale to some pilgrims on their way to Canterbury.

In the Middle Ages, in spite of the difficulties of travel,
it was common for Christians to make pilgrimages to
Jerusalem and other holy places. In England the most
popular of these was the shrine of St Thomas à Becket in
Canterbury Cathedral. Canterbury is less than sixty
miles from London, but on the muddy and pot-holed tracks
that in those days passed for roads it was a three or four
days' ride on horseback.

Chaucer's pilgrims came from all ranks of society and
included a noble Knight, an amorous young Squire, a
Prioress with worldly tastes, a jolly and much married
Wife of Bath, a studious Scholar, a bawdy Miller, a Cook,
a devout Parish Priest, and the Franklin. They all met at
the Tabard Inn at Southwark, where they decided to have
a competition to see who could tell the best story on the
journey. They were the sort of people that Chaucer met
in his busy daily life. He was a man of the world and had,
in the course of his life, been a serving soldier, a diplomat,
and Controller of Customs in the Port of London.
Shrewdly observant, humorous and good-natured, he was
himself one of the pilgrims.

Chaucer's language, usually known as Middle English,
is witty, forceful and direct, but it makes difficult reading
today. So I have retold the Franklin's Tale in modern
English, and in prose instead of in verse.

IAN SERRAILLIER

In Brittany there was once a knight called Arviragus. He loved a lady and did everything in his power to win her. She was the most beautiful lady under the sun and came of so noble a family that he didn't dare to tell her how much he loved her. But she understood his feelings. After a while she took pity on him and agreed to have him as her lord and master – as far as a husband can ever be called the master of his wife. He in his turn promised never to be jealous, or to force her to do anything against her will; but, for the sake of appearances, he would be called master.

Dorigen (for that was her name) thanked the knight and said, "Sir, as you have been so generous to me, I promise all my life to be a true and humble wife." And they lived harmoniously together. If there's one thing you can be sure of, it's this – a love that is to last cannot be forced. Once try to force it and it claps its wings and

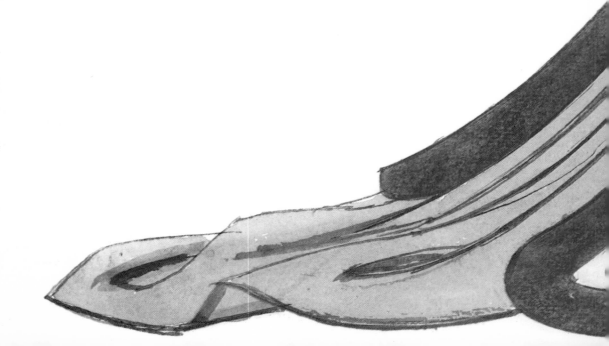

flies away. So the agreement between them was a sensible one, and he took her home to his own country, where they settled down contentedly together.

After a year or so Arviragus decided to go to England
to seek honour and glory in deeds of arms. He was away
for two years.

Dorigen, who loved him with all her heart, was very distressed by his absence. She couldn't eat or sleep. She wept, she pined for him, as good wives always do when their husbands are away. Her heart so ached for him that the world meant nothing to her, and she would not be comforted. With the arrival of letters from Arviragus, she recovered some of her spirits and at last agreed to leave her room and go out walking with her friends.

Now her castle stood near the sea, and she often liked to walk along the cliff top and watch the ships sailing by. But as she watched them, her sorrow came surging back, and she would cry, "Is there no ship among all these to bring my husband home and ease the pain in my heart?" And her eyes would fill with tears. At other times she would sit and think and gaze sadly down at the sea and say, "Eternal God, whose wisdom guides the world, didst Thou create these dark grisly rocks? A hundred thousand men – men whom Thou madest in Thine own image – have perished here. Oh, keep my husband safe! These rocks kill my heart with fear. I wish they were sunk into

hell." And she would weep bitterly. Then her friends, noticing that the sea only made her grief worse, led her inland to springs and rivers and other places of delight, where they danced and played games.

One morning early in May, they went to a garden near by to picnic and spend the day. Gentle showers had painted every leaf and flower, bringing out their scents

and colours. It was a paradise of beauty. After dinner they danced and sang, except for Dorigen, who sat by herself, wishing that her husband were there to dance with her.

Among the dancers was a young squire called Aurelius. He was brighter and more finely dressed than the month of May itself. No one since the world began had ever sung and danced as well as he. He was strong, handsome, rich, wise and talented, and everyone thought highly of him. But unfortunately, quite unknown to her, he had fallen in love with Dorigen. He had not dared to tell her, but for two years had kept his suffering and despair to himself. Only the songs and ballads he composed gave any hint of his feelings; and though he sang them in her presence, she never guessed their true meaning.

Well, it happened that he got talking with her and, seizing his chance, he told her of his love.

"Madam," he said, "I wish I had gone to England with Arviragus and never returned. I know that my devotion to you is hopeless, and all I shall get from it is a broken heart. Have pity on me. One word from you can kill me or save me. Oh, I wish I could die now at your feet!"

Dorigen was astounded. "Do you really mean this?" she said. "I had no idea. Now I know how you feel. But, by God who gave me life, I swear I will never be an unfaithful wife. That is my final answer." And she added jokingly, "Since you are so upset, I'll agree to be your

love on one condition. You must first remove all these rocks, stone by stone, from one end of Brittany to the other, so that they are no longer a danger to ships. Clear the coast completely, till not a single stone is left, and I'll promise to love you better than any other man."

"Is this all the mercy you can show me?" he said.

"Yes, by the Lord that made me! For I know very well that the task is impossible. So forget this foolishness."

"It is indeed impossible," said Aurelius, and away he went.

Soon Dorigen's friends rejoined her, and they wandered

up and down the garden till nightfall – or (as a poet might put it) "till the horizon had robbed the sun of its light." Then they went happily home.

But Aurelius was far from happy. Back in his house, he fell to his knees in despair and began to pray to the gods, especially to Apollo the sun god. "Lord Apollo, god of every plant and tree and flower, have pity on me. Ask your radiant sister Lucina, queen of the sea, to do a miracle. You know how she loves to be lit and kindled at your fire, and how she obeys your will as the tides obey her. Ask her at the next full moon to send a flood, a tide so high that it will submerge the highest rock in Brittany five fathoms deep. Let the moon stay at full and the high tide continue night and day for two years. Then I can say to my lady, 'Keep your promise. The rocks have gone.' Oh, Lord Apollo, see how the tears are streaming down my cheeks. Have pity on my pain!"

At once he fell into a swoon. His brother found him still unconscious and carried him off to bed.

Soon after this Arviragus came home, full of honour and glory, and at last Dorigen could clasp him in her arms. There was much dancing and merry-making.

Aurelius took no part in this. For two years he lay ill in bed, in great distress. All this time he had only his brother to listen to the tale of his troubles and to comfort him. His brother, who was a scholar, remembered a book

of magic which he had once seen in Orleans during his student days. A friend of his, a bachelor of law, had hidden it in his desk. There was a lot in the book about the working of the twenty-eight mansions of the moon, and other nonsense that no one believes nowadays. At the thought of this book his heart danced for joy, and he said to himself: "My brother will be cured. I'm sure a magician could conjure up all kinds of miraculous scenes – perhaps a lion, or a vineyard, or flowers in a field, or a barge rowing up and down – and he could make them vanish whenever he pleased, for none of them would be real. Why shouldn't he for a week or two make it look as if the grisly rocks of Brittany had vanished, and ships could come and go in safety along the coast? Then my brother would be cured, and the lady would have to keep her promise."

Well, to cut the story short, Aurelius and his brother

set off at once for Orleans. Just outside the town they met a young scholar, who greeted them in Latin and said, "I know why you've come here," then gave them the right answer straight away. Only a magician could have managed that.

Aurelius dismounted from his horse, and the magician

took them to his house and put them at their ease. Before supper he conjured up some amazing sights – parks full of wild deer, hawks killing a heron, knights jousting on a plain, and finally Dorigen herself dancing – and her partner seemed to be Aurelius! Then the magician clapped his hands, and the whole entertainment vanished. There

were just the three of them there, sitting in the study, and they had seen all these marvels without ever leaving the house.

After supper they discussed how much the magician should be paid for removing all the rocks of Brittany. He swore he wouldn't take less than a thousand pounds.

"What's a thousand pounds?" said Aurelius gaily. "I'd give the whole wide world, if it were mine to give. That's a bargain, then. You'll be paid in full, I promise."

Aurelius slept well that night. In the morning at daybreak he and the magician went straight back to Brittany.

It was the cold and frosty season of December. Bitter frosts, with sleet and rain, had destroyed the green in every garden. The sun was old and thinly shining – the colour of pale copper, no longer the burnished gold of full summer.

Encouraged by Aurelius, the magician started at once on his experiments – or, shall I say, his conjuring tricks? I'm afraid I know nothing whatever about centres and angles, proportionals, and all the rest of his astrological nonsense.

At last everything was ready; the right moment had arrived. So powerful was the spell the magician made that, whisht! all the rocks seemed to vanish; not one of them was left.

Night and day Aurelius had waited in anguish for this miracle. He fell to his knees and thanked the magician. Then off he went to look for Dorigen.

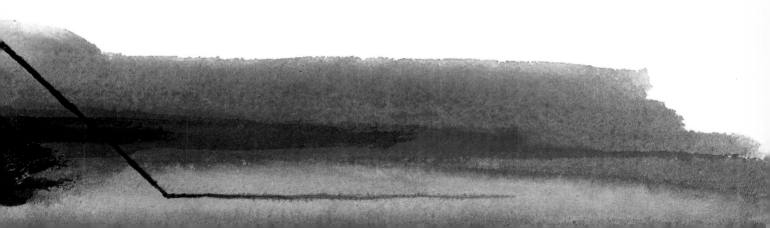

He found her in the temple and greeted her with trembling heart. "My own true lady," he said, "I've done what you commanded – all the rocks of Brittany have disappeared. Go and see for yourself." And he left her.

Home she went, so dismayed and frightened she could hardly walk.

Arviragus came home and found her in tears. When he asked her why she was weeping, the tears fell all the faster, and she told him all that I've been telling you. There's no need for me to say it all over again.

"All may yet be well," said her husband, calmly. "But

a promise is a solemn thing. You must keep it and accept your situation. I will bear my sorrow as best I can." And he burst into tears. Then he called a squire and maidservant to him. "Go with Dorigen," he said, "and take her wherever she tells you."

Dorigen knew now where she must go, and off she went into the town with her two puzzled attendants. In the middle of a crowded street she met Aurelius, who greeted her gaily and asked where she was going.

"To the garden to keep my promise, as my husband bade me," she said, distractedly.

Aurelius began to wonder. She looked so sad, and he felt so sorry for her, as well as for Arviragus, who had acted so chivalrously. Such generosity and nobility of mind were infectious.

"Madam," he said, "your distress and your husband's goodness touch my heart. Tell him that I would rather suffer agony for ever than destroy the love between you both. I release you from every promise you have made to me. And now I say goodbye to the best and truest lady I have ever known."

She knelt and thanked Aurelius, then went home to her husband. You can imagine how overjoyed he was. He and Dorigen lived together supremely happy for the rest of their lives. Never did an angry word pass between them, and she was true to him for ever. . . . That's enough now about those two.

What about Aurelius? He had lost everything, and he cursed the day he was born. "Oh, I wish I'd never promised that magician a thousand pounds in gold. I'm ruined. What am I to do? I'll have to sell my inheritance and go begging in the streets. I can't stay here and bring disgrace on all my family. I wonder if he'd let me pay off my debt, a little at a time. I'll go and ask him. Whatever happens, I'll keep my promise."

Gloomily he went to his treasure chest and took out some five hundred pounds in gold, which he brought to the magician, begging him to be generous and give him time to pay the rest. "Master, I've never yet failed to keep a

promise. I'll pay my debt to you, even though I have to go begging, with nothing but a shirt to my back. But if you could give me – on security – two or three years in which to pay, then I could manage it.''

"Haven't I kept my bargain with you?" said the magician.

"Yes, indeed you have."

"And haven't you enjoyed your lady's love?"

"No, no," he answered mournfully.

"Why not?"

Then Aurelius told him the whole story – but I won't weary you by going through it all again. "Dorigen made her promise in all innocence; she'd never heard of magical illusions. I felt so sorry for her that I was as generous to her as her husband was to me – I sent her back to him."

"Dear brother," said the magician, "you all behaved nobly to each other. Well, you're a squire and he's a

knight; I'd like to think a magician can behave as nobly too. Sir, I release you from your thousand pounds. It shall be the same as if we'd never met. I won't take a penny from you for my skill or my labour. You've paid for my board, and that's enough. Goodbye."

He mounted his horse and rode away.

And that's the end of my story. . . . But just a moment! I'd like to ask you a question: which of them seems to you the most generous?